COLLECTION OF THOUGHTS

Volume I

by

Wilbert E. August II

DORRANCE
PUBLISHING CO
EST. 1920
PITTSBURGH, PENNSYLVANIA 15238

Dorrance Publishing Co
585 Alpha Drive
Suite 103
Pittsburgh, PA 15238
Visit our website at *www.dorrancebookstore.com*

ISBN: 979-8-88729-243-4
eISBN: 979-8-88729-743-9

CONSIDER

Consider everything that has been shown.

To this condition, I declare it rare;

I know nothing yet my voice knows to groan.

Forgive, for which I dare not to compare,

Consider my ill views from the shadows

I glare your smiles, with envy I spite,

All seem glee, those plagued by Cupid's arrows.

When all is done I shift to the moonlight

To the world is it wrong, hear my desire?

Free? I have no time I can freely spend,

Nor the services you seem to require

Being a slave I have nothing, but tend.

I wait for Winter to come to an end

In hopes in Spring my love shall come again

A SILENT YET GODLY CHEER

Walking down the aisle there was no one behind me, no one leading me; it was only me; it was me who had to create my own path this time. My parents were away from the hall, but my passion awaited me on that vast, quiet stage. There she was, a pure grand piano welcoming me into her arms; her polished wood glowed under the fading stage lights. The countless stories she must have witnessed, incredible. To my left I saw the four judges scattered across the concert hall almost blending into the darkness. *I cannot fail my family,* I anxiously thought to myself. I grew closer to the stage until I faced the beauty of a Yamaha Grand. My heart began to race in syncopated beats. I took my seat, and my heart began to relax and crawled its way into a steady pace of comfort. I faced the four ambiguous judges and announced my name with pride flooded with naive confidence. It was mostly terror. In my fingers I had thirteen years of preparation; I was a veteran of this instrument. Sonata in F Major No. 1 III Movement was my introduction piece; this piece's commanding bass erupted the stage and shook the hall to its core. Capitalizing on Beethoven's masterful mixture of tense and dramatic melodies guided my hand like an artist's brush on an empty canvas. An electrifying piece to grab their attention, the bass alluded to a thunderous storm advancing on the beauty of nature and the right-hand melodic tone captured the panic of nature itself thrown into a panic. An abrupt end. The judges remained mute and signaled for the next piece. *Did they enjoy it, was I good enough?* Following the thunderous clouds of nature captured by Beethoven, I prepared to perform Chopin's Polonaise No 3 in A Major, The Militaristic Polonaise. Yet another thunderous introduction with the bass blasting octaves while the melody pranced across the whole piano like a drunk. The patriotic, clear, disciplined sounds illustrated a march of troops preparing to defend their home from invaders with hundreds of civilians cheering on their march to glory. The thunderous roars of the octaves, the cannon bombardment in the right hand depicted a battle, a ferocious battle that was agonizing on the hands, yet soothing to the ears. *A single cough, signaled the end of the song, no cheers, no applause, what am I doing wrong?* I grew weary, my fingers began to waver. The Grand sang her last note as I raised in front of the judges of the hall like a phoenix and announced my ambitions, my dreams in the form of a song. By the time I reunited with my family in another hall, it was announced that my sound had reached the judges, they heard and understood my message, my desires. A silent cheer from my parents as we returned to the car, but it was a Godly cheer from the heavens within my heart as I came, I saw, and I conquered.

RETURNING TO THE LIGHT OF DAY

They asked me for my name, birth date, and any other basic form of identification while handing my belongings I drug into this place eight months prior. Has the world forgotten about the child named Will August born and raised in Dallas? This lingering parasite was glued in my aching head as I took those long, echoing steps down the quiet, vacant hall. To believe it'd been eight sluggish months since I woke up strapped in a hospital where I was more machine than human, eight long months I was away from the eyes of the public hidden away like a caged, injured beast. As I inched closer to the exit sign, time began to slumber as my legs grew weaker with every step; my anxiety grew as I was not prepared to face the unknown. Not knowing was a nightmarish thought. What had changed while I was gone, had I changed enough, had the world forgotten who I was, had I forgotten who I was? Nonetheless, I marched to the rhythm of my chest and held my head high, knowing that I had cheated the Grim Reaper. Yes, I was able to escape the jaws of death and now I must face my future like a lion. I met the exit door. The door opened slowly, and the sun was the first to welcome my eyes. Finally, I thought to myself. My mother embraced me, the old me, and the current me, and the future me all at once. I whispered to her as I felt a small tear escape from my eyes. I was ready to be free once again. The road to recovery was complete, and yet the road to my new life has just begun. Mom, I love you so much.

SIMPLE

It was simple, I miss you. However, it felt like I didn't know you or understand your story. It was simple. I loved you—I think. As a child it is hard to comprehend the idea of death; the end of a life might be a new beginning, or it just might be the end of everything. Is it scary to take your final breath? Are you cold? Can you hear me? I guess not. Hey, Grandma, can you please just answer one of my questions before you go? Did you hear the last time I said I love you? Can you please just move one more time, can you just hug me one more time? Can you sing my favorite song before I go to bed one more time? I can't do it alone. Hey, please wake up. It's simple, just wake up. Fuck.

TODAY

Death is a universal law, but there are two kinds of Death in our society: Death from the external world and Death from the internal demons. To be born is a Death sentence that we are unaware of at an early age, because we are naive, we are idiots who think that life is a journey where tragedy is a rarity. To be born is an ironic tragedy, because once we are aware of who we are, we realize that time will always move forward, leaving every one of us behind, no matter a person's race, financial standing, height, wisdom, or skill. Writing this, it pains me that I have to remind you of our punishment for being born, but what if that is what makes life so worth living? The fact that Death is within us all and the fact that we are unaware when our demise will take place maybe, just maybe, that is what makes life so precious. To live forever is just watching the memories you create die as you move forward with time, but because we all have an end, we are forced to cherish things because the unknowing strikes fear in every human's heart.

I'm going to fucking do it. I'm going to fucking do it! That simple, six-worded phrase was the only justification John needed to end his six-year war of terror. There was no metaphor, there was no color behind those words—it was just black and white. His car was flooded with the smell of alcohol, John was a rum type of guy, so you could imagine the rodent odor of rum sitting in the oven like the heat of Florida for days at a time, yet he smelled nothing unusual. The smell of rum was a prelude of another night of drinking alone, so his brain fell in love with the aroma of the Devil's juice. Mixed in his car was the presence of marijuana and cigarettes (both the literal and electric devices). His car was just a dungeon for anyone's nose. It was John's escape from reality, his twisted sanctuary. Unfortunately, the distinguished smells of his paradise was no longer a sanctuary on December 10. It was John's designated coffin. With every dismal chug of rum, John sank further with his demon; with every puff, his lungs gasped for air not knowing their brain had decided to end operations of them. His coffin was a normal 2016 white Kia Optima that was on her last legs just as her owner was—on the outside she seemed fine, but on the inside, it was a chaotic, yet organized, pile of shit.

Oh… looks like I finished my last bottle of rum, John thought to himself as he emptied the last remainder of booze engulfing his liver in a tug of war with death. Things were not looking good for him, and he knew it. Mozart's requiem in D minor began to play on the radio as if God and Lucifer signaled it was time for him to commit the greatest sin known to man: the destruction of God's greatest creation. He inched his way to the glove box of his beaten Kia, his mind stood still, his heart slowly realized it was time and hurled blood throughout his body in a panic. One gun, one bullet, one man, one demon. It was simple to a defeated man; it didn't have to make sense to everyone or even anyone; it made sense to him. As he loaded his gun, the phone woke up from its slumber. It was Carol. *How did I get to this point?* John muttered as he looked back on his day, where it all began in his condo.

A slave to his routine, that is what John has become. Every morning at 8:00 a.m., his energetic, demonic, tabby cat Scrappy would engage in her rampage across the condo. Pouncing on every couch, every table, even her shadow was not safe from her barrage of attacks. He always set his alarm for 8:30 a.m. to prepare for his work at the office, but the cat always had other plans attacking John as if he were a mouse. *Today is the day*, John thought to himself as one eye glared at his phone, his mind was still prancing in the wonderland of his dreams. Usually, he would wash his face with Hydro Boost clean, brush his (already white) teeth, prepare his black curly hair, pick an outfit for the day, grab some breakfast, and crawl his way to his work. Unknowingly to the world, today was the day; no work meant no routine for the day—John stayed in bed past 8:30 a.m.

It was noon, that's what John at least thought the time was, when the slumbering fool finally awakened from the fairytale-like dream. Of course, with Scrappy right by his side. She was hungry and confused about the fact her owner's routine was not in place; that's what John at least assumed his cat thought at the time as he carried her to the kitchen so they could both enjoy breakfast. He didn't wash his face with Hydro Boost, instead he used the last remaining of his lotion, he didn't brush his teeth, opting for just mouthwash this morning. He didn't brush his hair and for breakfast all he had was water. Instead of heading to his day-to-day office job, John had three locations in mind: the liquor store, the armory outside of his Floridian town, and the local dispensary.

Today was the day, today was the day John would finally claim victory over his Demon, today was the day that John could finally peacefully rest. John noticed his phone was on silent, that quickly changed before he left to start his final day on Earth.

Usually, the highway was packed like sardines, bumper to bumper, honking and yelling in the distance with the sun waking from its slumber, but it was noon. The roads were still. There was no yelling or honking; instead John was able to fly past other cars utilizing the right lane as if he were a character from *Mad Max*. The first stop was the liquor store. The poisonous beverage was a popular friend of the Thomas' family: it enslaved John, his father Baker, two of his uncles, and his grandfather. John was the only one alive. He never met his father, never heard stories about his grandfather, watched one uncle commit suicide, and the other died while drinking and driving a few years back. Baker, a rum lover, his two uncles, Bill and Phil, died by rum, and his grandfather Mark engulfed rum like it was water. *I think rum should be my beverage of choice. Maybe an IPA or two.* John thought to himself as he inched his way off the highway, with the liquor store in sight. His liver shriveled with fear as the sight of the liquor store grew in size. His phone buzzed in his pocket as he parked the car; he returned the phone to silent—he didn't even bother to check who was on the other side. Within the next 24 hours John Thomas was going to become a memory, a victim to his own demise or a victim of sexual assault, or abuse. Whatever the case, John the Victim of Florida was prepared to leave without saying goodbye.

"John?" The clerk's voice hiccupped as he couldn't believe his eyes. John was a regular on a Saturday who always showed up at 11 a.m. on the dot. Everyone in the town knew about his routine, but today was a Wednesday. And there was John at his liquor store and not at work.

"John, what can I do for you today?"

"Frankie, how are you doing? How's my favorite liquor store holding up?" John patrolled around the whole store, but he knew what he was looking for. Two bottles of Captain Morgan 100 proof, but it seemed John wanted to chat to Frankie for a while. There was no one else in the store.

"I'm living, my wife and I just had our first kid. Aren't you supposed to be at work right now? It's only 1 p.m.?" asked

Frankie, his voice began to waver as things were not adding up.
"Boy or girl?"

"Girl."

"Name?"

"Natalia, Natalia Smith."

"What a precious name, I might make a poem called Natalia Smith dedicated to the importance and blessing that life is!"

"Why aren't you at work, John?"

"You want to hear my poem that just got published?" asked John as he approached the register with his two bottles of rum. Ignoring all of Frankie's questions about work, he proceeded to pull out his phone and began to recite his most recent work that gained worldwide recognition. A series of poems called *Life of Poet*:

Birth

To be welcomed, two beings I know not I cry,
I scream from darkness, I see light.
A newborn flower blooms, a sight they thought;
Spite of me they smile, fearful I might
To be named, I understand not a sound
I squirm like a bug as I learn movement
They smiled, this infant fool who was crowned the
peaceful fresh air, what an improvement
Who am I, what am I, Why was I born?
Struggle to breathe, should I exist with ease?

Another life is given, shall we mourn?
Who allowed me to exist, this disease?
I was picked to be born, a tragedy
To be, I hold a soul of agony.

Life
I am who I am, I am what I am
I; nothing more than a swarm of atoms
Poisoned by the plague, follow thy program
I wish to hide, my vision like Tatum's
It is hard to live a life, to be free the world says be happy,
to yell for joy Isn't life marvelous, don't you agree?
Conquer life, like the men who conquered Troy!
Just be happy, just make friends they all say
Just live your life we all only have one
Just take this fucking world on day by day
Just be; don't be another anyone
For those who preach to me of better times
I must pray to God; prepare for my crimes

Suicide
I sit here, knowing I am doomed to hell
I sit here not as your equal, never.
I sit here, preparing for my dispel
I sit here, welcome, darkness forever
I pray to you as I write my farewells

I ask for your forgiveness I beg, Lord
I wish I could enjoy the season bells
But my cries, my pain, all of it; ignored
I sit here with nothing more than a gun
I sit here, I rest my pen for the end
I sit here, yearning for the holy sun
I sit here, knowing my soul will descend
To say I have failed as your creation
I hereby sentence thee to damnation

Death
The act, done, my final poem complete
I fall to the flames as I watch Cobain
The world of fire, what awaits this heat
At last maybe I am free from thy pain
Nero, Bennington, Robin, and now I
We all fell to our demise, suicide
I beg the world of the living, don't cry
I killed myself, while having zero pride
What caused this, why would one choose to die, why?
Ask my body, ask the dead why this fate.
All of you, everyone, you, just stood by
Now you ask, you ask, I disintegrate
I wish I could be or what If I knew
To look at me I should yell, I love you

Frankie could only stand in awe of the raw, daring performance John portrayed as if he were an orator from the ancient Greek world. The amount of courage and emotions embedded in a short piece only captivated him even more. It was pure beauty without any adjustment or editing, just pure art.

"You know what, John, you can have the two bottles for free because that was beautiful, but only on one condition. If you tell me who the poem is about," said Frankie as he tucked the bottles in the brown bags.

"Here's 45 dollars, Frankie, keep the change."

Getting back in his Kia, John decided to check his phone. Work called him twice in hopes of getting those reports that were due three days ago; his mom called twice. Maybe it was about Carol or his cat or just wanting to say hi. An NBA trade and a missed call from Carol. The phone was put back to silent mode and buried away in the glove department; with one destination down, John began to feel uneasy. A step closer to his freedom, right? That is what he has been preaching to himself. Or is that what HE preached to John? Was John really in control or was HE the one following the teachings of Hitler by creating fear and using it as a mechanism to control him like a slave? The next stop was the armory store located just outside of his town, about a 20-minute drive, but it seemed the clouds grew envious of the sun's freedom. Nature's aroma shifted, a storm formed a couple of towns over and headed towards him. *Guess I'll pour myself a small glass of rum* (neat, of course) *and listen to some music before I head off,* John thought to himself as his mother's favorite song came on the radio. *At Last* by Etta James smothered the parked car as John sipped on his rum. An image of his late father dancing with his mother appeared in his foggy mind. *I should call her before we say goodbye,* John thought to himself. **You will only be a burden just like your father was, a useless tragedy,** he whispered as the image of his father's casket paraded around his mind.

The clock read 2:45 pm; the rain danced on the car in a steady beat as the romantic ballad came to an end. In the brief moment of silence, his phone screamed in the glovebox of his car begging to breathe. *I guess it's time to leave,* John whispered to himself as drove off towards the highway, headed straight for the storm. It was lunch hour for those stuck in a box called work, packing the highways like hotdogs shoved together in a small package. A 25-minute drive quickly became a 45 minute one. The drive was a grueling, quiet, 40-minute drive. It was nothing out of the ordinary: a middle finger there, a scream there, an accident or two—this was American highways for you. The phone rang again. It was Carol.

"Look, you haven't answered any of my texts! Where have you been?" asked Carol as she marched to her car preparing to try the new salad buffet place that opened across the street. It was her lunch break; she recently started a diet.

"I've been busy. Around town."

"Why aren't you at the office? Weren't we supposed to present our proposal?"

"I sent you the files, check your email," declared John as the armory came to his sight.

I need to tell her to check her message board just in case- maybe I shouldn't bring it up to her, John thought to himself as he parked his vehicle in front of the store.

"What do you—"

"Check your message board as well. I sent something else. Bye," said John.

The store seemed abandoned to those who didn't know the owner, but John was a regular here. Never bought a gun, but was intrigued with weapons—not a person to fear, just a man who wished to collect old firearms that stood the test of time. Again, there were only two cars in the lot as the storm raged on. *Damn, I wish I brought my umbrella or a fucking raincoat,* John thought to himself as he approached the dull building. *Another broken window, Jesus Brady,* John whispered to himself.

"John? What can I do for you today?" asked Brady as he checked his inventory—for some reason, around this time, sales went through the roof. Actually, to John's surprise, this was the only time this abandoned place saw any business, but this old man still pushed through.

"Hey Brady, all I need is a GLOCK G19—nothing too fancy," John replied as he stalked along the isles like a pack of lions circling around their victim. "No shooting range today?" asked Brady "No," John simply replied.

The awkward silence between the two men was interrupted by John's phone—once again, it was Carol, but this time there were no text messages before the call. *Guess I should answer this one just in case*, John thought to himself. **"No,"** John's mind shouted.

"So John, have you been attending your sessions with your therapist and taking your medication? Your mother is worried."

"No."

"So no medication, no sessions, not at the office, and here you are in my gun store," questioned Brady as he gawked at John.

"Get to the fucking point, Brady, are you going to sell me this gun or not?" demanded John.

"As a friend no, but as a business owner, I'm obligated to," responded Brady.

"Thank you."

"What would Carol think, John?"

"How about you go ask her, old man? Keep the change, by the way."

That fucking Brady always in my god damn business, always asking the questions about my private life, my family, my issues; doesn't he have his own problems? Like that fucking broken window that he stares at all day, John pondered to himself as he stormed out of the store. The storm had ceased, but the murky clouds lingered over the town. The Florida town lost its dreamlike sunshine as

John sat in his car planning his last trip. Unfortunately, the dispensary was closed due to personal reasoning of the manager, a devastating event that hindered John's final day on this floating rock. The clock read 4:12; it was time to feed the cat (supposed to feed the cat twelve minutes ago, actually). *Hopefully the roads aren't as busy this time*, John whispered to himself as he dragged his vehicle to the highway, his car full of interesting passengers: a man with a death wish, two bottles of rum, a GLOCK G19, and his phone that remained screaming in the glove compartment of the car.

Scrappy, the judgmental clown of a cat, stood at the door of the condo, displeased that her human was late for super. John bought her favorite food the night before and presented the dish for the cat; John's meal was a surf and turf dish. Medium rare steak topped with shrimp, paired with a creamy crab mashed potatoes, and of course, rice. The dining room table was cluttered: medication packages piled on the table which rivaled the mountain of Hiroshima in sheer size, the foreboding, foul pistol laid across the table (it tried to tease the man but to no avail), the two bottles of rum towered over the table overwatching the organized chaos that ran rampant across the dismal table. In front of John, however, was his food and his phone that slept quietly on silent mode, at this point it might have been on airplane mode.

"Daddy has to go to the parking garage across town, Scrappy," said John as he leaned over the table and cradled his cat. His breath reeked of alcohol, the sweet, spicy smell of rum of course, and his damped clothes were slippery due to the constant bombardment from the storm that besieged the town earlier.

The cat's greenish, childlike eyes stared into John's eyes that held no light. It pretended and behaved as if the cat understood this was the final farewell between the two.

Saying goodbye to a person is devastating for us humans, but saying goodbye to someone or something that can't understand that this goodbye is permanent is heartbreaking because we know they will never comprehend that this is the end.

"I love you so much, but Mommy is going to come get you tomorrow. See you next time… Well, I guess there is no next time," declared John as he sat the cat on her favorite chair.

The drive was quiet; none of the passengers in the car dared to utter a word (of course, the bottles, the gun, and cigs uttered a word); even the phone remained silent as John drove to the garage.

The garage was empty.

As John's Kia crept into the highest level and inched its way to a lonesome parking lot, John began to flood the contacts of his phones with goodbyes and farewells. Some were complex messages full of sorrow, regrets, and despair. While others were simply a two-word phrase that captured the final moments of his life, "*Goodbye Friend.*" John's phone decided to break the silence that plagued his car and shouted to the top of its lungs. It was Carol, the same woman who had harassed John all day. John answered the last call.

"Get out of the car, John, I got your message," she said as she parked her car right behind John's parked Kia.

"What do you mean—"

"I'm behind your car. Do you think I'm stupid? This was our favorite spot when we wanted to get away from the world," she said.

"Leave Carol, just get the fuck out of here," said John as he gripped his pistol in disbelief.

"Come and say it to me like a man and stop hiding."

John hung up the phone and stared at the dashboard of his car as his mind ran through the insanity of his situation that appeared. It was Carol, it was fucking Carol behind John. *I didn't want her to see me like this, I wanted her to think I was normal until it was too late,* John whispered to himself as he exited the vehicle. The gun was glued to his hand as his anxiety, anger, fear reached their boiling point. The emotions of it all engulfed John; the reality of his situation drowned the broken man. The one person he didn't want to see stood before him, a pathetic creature that was lost witnessed their beloved deity on his final night. *Why is she here?* he thought to himself as he turned off the safety.

"Put it away John, put that damn thing down now!" declared Carol as she inched across the parking garage. The garage was like a grave, desolate, and cold. The old structure smelled of rotten animals that engulfed their noses like poison.

"Carol, you know nothing, not a thing about me or him."

"I can help, I understand—"

"Help? You think you're some savior or some bullshit?" said John as he swung the gun to the side of his head, the barrel rested on his temple drenched in sweat.

"John, calm down, just relax—"

"Relax? Do you know what it's like to go to bed hoping you don't wake up? Do you!"

"No, I don't."

"Yet here you are saying you can save me. Don't waste your time on someone who already wasted their own."

Just let me fucking go! Over and over and fucking over you appear—stop holding on to me, John thought to himself.

"You're wrong."

"How?"

"You kept that phone on you in hopes someone would call you. You want to be found, you want to be heard, but you don't know how to ask it, damn it!" yelled Carol as a lonely tear fell from her boorish cheek.

Anger is what drives a man to do the unthinkable, we are not born killers, we don't want to witness others in pain, we want to live. This raw emotion can blind us from those that are willing to take our pain as if it were their own.

"Shut the hell up, you don't know shit."

"Denial, that's all you do. Even now, you are in denial that I am here in front of you," she said as she glared at him, reaching for his hand.

Like hell she was going to leave this garage without John within her arms even if it meant she had to beat him to pulp.

Damn it Carol, I am just tired.

Please God, let me take John home with me.

Finally reaching John, she embraced the impaired soul of John; she grabbed the gun and lowered it from his head. The safety was never turned off. Carol finally reached John and John finally allowed himself to view the world for what it is. A place of uncertainty, tragedy, failures, dangers, and destruction, and yet it is still a beautiful balance with the ones we love and cherish. That is what makes life a special type of beauty; it is far from perfect and has its flaws, but every day we are able to find joy in sorrow, light in darkness, as long as we have those that love us unconditionally.

Today was the day that John found his Carol; today was the day that John determined that his last day would remain a mystery to him forever.

DEAR GOD IT'S FRIDAY

"Did you have all of your homework done, did you brush your teeth and wash them underarms, young man?" preached Tucker's mom as she cleans the young man's new shoes before his big day. The two have seen their victories from Tucker winning the Plymouth Spelling Bee, to witnessing the horrors life can throw at you. From the dull days of winter to the explosive days of summer, side by side the two have witnessed it all.

"Mom, the phone is ringing in the kitchen!" screamed the young Tucker, vigorously playing *Halo 3* with his best friends from school. It was his normal routine on dark, rainy nights on a cool weekend; however today was the big middle school dance.

"Hello, yes, this is the Field residence. How may I help you?" I remember that night, the cold illusive winds coming from the north crashed against our old, beaten windows, calmly whistling their eerie tunes. The harmonies were not of death or misery, no, it was more of a lonesome lullaby supported by the vibration of dry leaves.

"Tucker, can you please turn off the game?" Her voice was skipping beats, tears building up in her eyes.

"Mom, wait, I'm almost done with this level," Tucker calmly responded. It was too early, it wasn't even dinner yet, Tucker thought to himself. Even Dad wasn't home for dinner yet, and he is never late for dinner.

"Tucker, please tur—" Tucker's mom pleaded.

"But, Mom please—"

"TUCKER, TURN OFF THE DAMN GAME NOW!" Mrs. Field shouted, her yell echoing throughout the walls of the old home silencing all who could hear.

The damaged mother of one, the wife of Parker Field, the relaxed third grade teacher reduced to a damaged woman embracing her son. The rain grew stronger with every moment that slipped by. Dancing on our windows, the winds began to pick up tempo and the old trees of the field began to bash and crash into the sides of the home.

"Tucker, your father is gone, your father is gone." She dropped to her knees holding her son, her soul shattered by the memories of the smile that she married, never to hold him again. That was the day my daddy died.

"So Tucker, who's the lucky girl?" Doing a final clean down on the boy's new, expensive red tux paired with a white slick black bow tie, she took a look at her seventeen-year-old son. Anyone could tell just how proud she was of her young man just by witnessing that soft, gentle smile. That's Patrick's smile, she thought to herself.

"Her name is Diana," he replied softly.

It was obvious the widowed mother of one had an ocean of worries that engulfed her imagination—will I be able to pay the bills, is he doing great in school, would I be able to afford college and support his dream, will there be enough food on the dinner table? And now this, a major change of pace for her son. Not only was he facing the battles of education, music, sports, handling friendships, but now he was diving into the mysterious, abstract world of young, innocent love.

"So what are you guys planning for the night, Tucker?" asked Ms. Field, gathering cash from her wallet.

"I am going to take her to the Seafood Palace," replied Tucker.

"Seafood Palace? You know that place is expensive and requires a reservation to get in on weekends, especially on Friday nights." She paused for a second, trying to calculate just how expensive this date was going to be. Did he need 60 dollars, 80 dollars, maybe 100 dollars, what if he needed more?

"I know, Mom, I know." Tucker laughed. "I already made a reservation and I have been saving up money from my part time job, so you don't have to give me any money." Tucker continued to try to calm his mother down who was literally a bomb of mixed emotions ranging from excitement to worry with a splash of fear of the unknowing. A constant war of emotions every parent faces while raising a child no matter the age, Ms. Field would exclaim.

"You already made reservations, what time is it?" She asked.

"10:30 p.m." Tucker smiled at his mom.

"Well, it's 9:30 p.m. right now, you should get going soon, don't you think?" Mrs. Field added, giving her son one last hug before he set off on his adventure.

"Make sure you drive safely out there, there's going to be a huge storm tonight, so make sure you follow the rules, no texting, 10-2 driving style like you learned at drivers ed, and no speeding." Ms. Field continued giving her son a last-minute speech that fell on deaf ears, but it only showed just how much she cares for her beloved son.

"I know, Mom, but I have to go pick her up. I can't be late on my first date." His smile was softer than any fabric, gentler than the furriest kitten, more innocent than a Saint. Parker, our son is becoming a man, a bright young man just like you, she thought to herself.

"Come here and give your mommy one last hug, dear." She embraced her son one last time before he departed for his first date. No, it wasn't a perfect Friday night, a storm was forming with malicious winds, but nothing could stop a man on a mission.

As Tucker left out the front door, his mother strolled to the couch to look over the family photos and listen to the family records. As time went by, the storm grew stronger and stronger to the point where the barrage of barbaric thunder began to clash on the windows as if a Demon were knocking on her door, begging for shelter. The clashes of thunder combined with the fanatical prancing of the rain started to bring up dark memories of that fateful day that was destroyed by a single phone call at around 10:20 p.m. It had been ten years, and yet Ms. Field was still struggling to get over the fact her one and only prince charming was gone in the wind.

Around 10:24 p.m., the phone in the kitchen started to ring. It was literally a repeat of that night ten years ago: the thunder, the rain, the time, the phone ringing, it was as if she were re-living that moment again. At first, she was hesitant to answer the phone, but she was able to draw up the courage to take the great leap.

"Hello, yes, this is the Field residence, how may I help you?" On the other end of the call, it was the same voice that called ten years ago.

"Hi, my name is Nurse West, is Tucker Field your son, Ms. Field?"

"Yes, that is my only child...." She replied, her voice was dragging its feet, her throat became dry, her heart rate steadily climbed Mt. Fuji.

"I'm sorry to tell you this, but your son died in a car acci-dent at around 10:20 p.m. We did all we could do; however, he had already passed by the time he arrived at the hospital. The passenger lived, but unfortunately, she is in critical condition."

"Thank you," she replied with no emotion.

"Do you want to know what happened?" The nurse asked.

"No. Thank you for calling, have a great Friday."

She threw the phone on the hardwood floor, shattering the object to pieces; the storm grew in strength. Ironically, Chopin's Funeral March began to play on the record player. The atmosphere grew dark, cold, distressed, screaming with agony while searching for hope, a hope she found in a knife. No one can imagine what was going through the once-widowed mother to now a mother without a child's mind; one could guess she began to question her existence, questioning her God.

She moved to the master bathroom, knife in hand, and laid in the empty tub.

"I'm coming home, my sweethearts," she thought to herself, before she committed the greatest sin in the Christian religion. Her blood slowly leaked into the tub as the Funeral March came to a close.

Dear God it's Friday again.

A NORMAL ROSE

Her eyes are nothing like the bleeding sun
A dying rose is more graceful than her lips
To say I love her while her breasts are dun
If our love is strong, then my greed eclipse
To say she's an angel a lie is born
Her hair is no smoother than this damned spike
I feel my damaged, broken heart is torn
To those who question her, I shall strike
I have seen roses gleaming of red and white
But no roses live on her boorish cheeks
Her smile is boring, has no delight
Even her smell rivals mine, it reeks
By chance alone I feel our love is rare
No one dare to say their love can compare

MY WIFE IS HERE

Spring is the gateway to summer, a beautiful time where nature awakens from her prolonged slumber. Her children begin to settle in the skyscraper of trees where homes of rigid, fresh bits of branches begin to rise, a place for the old to welcome the young.

"Two please," Mr. Greene humbly asked.

"Welcome back to the U.S.S. Michigan Mr. Greene. I have to say, I can't believe it's that time of the year again for you and your wife," responded the clerk in a familiar matter, for he has known Mr. Greene for the past twenty six years. When the calendar strikes, May 5th, Mr. and Mrs. Greene had created a tradition for the two to celebrate not only their anniversary, but also Ms. Greene's birthday by enjoying a simple, yet majestic ferry ride on the U.S.S. Michigan. A tradition that had lasted for thirty-one years now. No matter the cost, no matter the weather, tradition is tradition for the Greene family.

"Ah… Mr. Campell," responded the soft-spoken Mr. Greene showcasing, his delicate old smile. "I can't believe it's already May 5th. Between you and me, if it weren't for my wife, I would have almost forgotten since time is not bound by our human laws, the bastard can fly at any speed without a care for us," exclaimed Mr. Greene.

"Or… we're both climbing in age?" Mr. Campell fired back in a joking manner.

It was a perfect day to enjoy a peaceful ferry ride on the river. The water was calm and gentle as if it were in a deep slumber, dreaming of what it would be like to be born in an ocean, the trees rocked along to the songs of the southern winds. It was spring, so of course the newborn leaves began to join in adding their own musical elements to nature's tune. It was around seven o'clock when the sun's orange and fiery red blood gushed out onto the clouds; it was as if the scene Mr. and Mrs. Green witnessed thirty-one years ago. Times may have changed, but the beauty had not.

"That will be twelve dollars, Mr. Greene," stated Mr. Campbell.

"Of course, of course. Did you know these tickets used to cost two dollars for two people?" exclaimed Mr. Green while handing the clerk three fresh five-dollar bills.

"I wish those days are today, your total change is three dol—"

"You should know this by now, Campbell, you put those three dollars in your pocket, we have been doing this for almost three decades now," asserted Mr. Greene while slipping the clerk an extra few dollars.

"My thanks, Mr. Greene."

The clock struck 7:15 p.m. and right on cue, the bells on the ferry signaled the ship's departure into the still sleeping river. The clerk and the elderly couple shared their final words until it was time to board. The two rushed into the ship as if it were 1958 once again, where the bells had rung on their final days of high school, Mr. and Mrs. Greene leaped into the hands of summer once again.

"Enjoy the boat ride, Mr. Greene!" shouted Mr. Campbell.

As the couple explored the crumbling little ferry boat as if it were not their thirty-first time aboard the little ship, nothing much had changed since their first exploration decades ago. The bar still offered the same drinks, the halls were decorated with the same paintings by the same artist, the tables in the ball-room were still arranged in the same way with all the wool-covered tables gathered around a center stage for performers and musicians to amaze the crowds. Mr. Greene stumbled upon the bow of the boat where guests were treated to luxurious music along with nature's paintings. As he pulled up two chairs from behind him, he could hear the delicate songs of the piano resonate throughout the ship. Beautiful, no. Magnificent, maybe or was it euphoric. As the ship began to head south, the comforting, homey winds began to invade the bow of the ship embracing not only the ancient ferry but also the guests who were blessed to be on the bow, witnessing nature's warmth.

"John Field's Nocturne No. 5 in B flat Major," announced the pianist.

As the piano began to sing with perfect harmony, Mr. Greene was caught in a brief moment of untainted happiness. The clouds painted in a soft coat of orange with a splash of fiery red, the crashing of the slumbering river against the sides of the old beaten boat, the sun slowly fading away behind the clouds, the winds dancing with the leaves, this is God's perfect painting, his perfect creation. Nature itself. Directly above the boat was a flock of birds chatting among themselves as they soared through the sky. The type was unknown to Mr. Greene, but as he gazed upon the innocent beings, a thought occurred to the old, decaying man.

Is this what Heaven sounds like… looks like… feels like… is this the meaning of perfection? Questioning this to himself, Mr. Greene rose from his chair and took a deep breath of fresh air as an isolated tear began to escape from him. As he looked over the ship, his memories began to fill the river: the day he met his charming wife, Mary Kaitlyn; the day his first son, Phillip Greene, was born; the day his mother passed away; the day he became a grandfather, and the war. All of it came to him again as he, in his own opinion, experienced his first true "perfection."

As the piano slowly began to fade away reaching its hushed resolution, a final breeze over swept Mr. Greene. This breeze, however, was not the usual chill feeling; it felt warm, familiar, welcoming, like home for some reason. He turned his body back to the two empty chairs he placed for him and his wife with no one beside him, no one behind him, no one to embrace him, no one to comfort him. Walking towards the piano as the keys screamed its final pitch, he handed the musician a hefty tip while leaning over and whispering to the musician, "That, my friend, is the closest thing to perfection…. My wife played that song every Sunday evening after we finished our family dinner. It was not the most complex piece she knew, but it was still her favorite," muttered Mr. Greene.

"I'm glad you enjoyed the performance. Is your wife with you?" asked the pianist as he began to pack his books away.

That was her favorite piece she played on the ole grand back home… Mr. Greene thought to himself as he pulled out an old photo of his deceased wife.

"Well… no, not really. She is, but at the same time, she isn't."

Slowly walking back to the bow of the small, delicate ferry ship, Mr. Greene took his final sip of his rum and Coke and gazed upon the clouds. The sun had fallen asleep and only the bright, eerie moon oversaw the ship from above. *It's been ten years since Cancer took her away… ten long, agonizing years,* Mr. Greene thought to himself as he leaned over the ship to witness the river's elegant dance.

"Happy anniversary to my beautiful wife… and a happy birthday to my angel. I love you," Mr. Greene whispered to himself as the ferry approached the harbor with Mr. Campbell waving from the shore, welcoming his return from his great voyage.

"Mr. Greene, how did you and your wife enjoy the ride?" asked Mr. Campbell as he helped the old man off the ship.

"I enjoyed the ride as always."

"And your wife?"

"She couldn't make it this year even if it's our tradition, but I'm sure the views from above aren't rivaled by anything this world could offer."

Tradition is tradition to the Greene family, no matter the cost, no matter the weather, no matter who is lost.

LACK OF

To say I believe faith shall guide us all,
For some their roads are blessed rather than dull.
In fear I witness my ungraceful fall
My eyes lurk thy beauty, wish to indulge.
Cupid's arrows continue to float by.
Every mission a compromise resides,
Quiet crowd, tired of this lullaby.
Memories multiply never divides
Nothing has really changed, only our age.
Want you to notice, when I'm not around.
Nothing has really changed, ask the old sage.
Want you to notice, when I'm not abound.
Love is something we seek to heal our wounds
Unfortunately, my pain just resumes

THE DANCE

Although it is morning, I sit in the dark. The sun bleeds through delicate curtains, illuminating my somber, bleak room. Impaled by questions I ponder my aching head, answers I wish had never come.

The dance has ended, yet there she is standing with command. I am afraid of her.

Her immoral two step strangled my lungs, depriving my mind of oxygen. A mist began to invade our tango, blocking the sun, clogging my heart. Her name was Mary.

Although it is night, I sit in the dark.

The curtains shut, a black parade swallows my fortress, only silence is welcomed. My crippled heart dances at a syncopated beat, the sweltering heat engulfs my demoralized brain.

My dismal room no longer welcomes me.

It devours me!

It seems that I alone understand her true nature.

The dance is over and yet there she is behind me, whispering the gospels of addiction.

She won't rest!

Our routine was simple, yet daring; fatal, yet delicate.

Those flirtatious, captivating movements hypnotized me, no, it possessed me. Was it love or was it a tragic tale of a man lured in by pleasure?

Although it is morning, I sit in the dark replaying those bloodcurdling terrors. Even though she no longer haunts me she follows me whispering—enslavement.

TALES OF AGONY:

THE LONELY DANCE

One, two, three... The room grew so quiet with every drip of tainted water that danced among the roaches and sang with the mole that masked the walls—a boy stared into the abyss with not a hint of life. His delicate, anguished mind consumed by the plague of man, despair. His spirit was nothing more than a shell of his youth, vigorously worshiping the Princes of Hell glorifying their dance of the dead. A slothful, hellish dance where those who dance shall do so until the King is pleased and banish thee to the flames. Fifty-three, fifty-four, fifty-five... The wind whispers against the windows begging for entrance to this dreadful ball, even the dying oak tree dares to stand firm; only a fool would ask for the next dance. Repeating the same steps in a hopeless loop, the boy's eyes illuminate the emptiness, the pain of what life brings to man. Seventy-six, seventy-seven, seventy-eight... "This dance requires two," exclaimed Persephone as the boy smiled, replying, "The only partner I need is silence, the beautiful sound of silence where no one can harm me again. Yes, this silence is my home." Ninety-eight… As time began to slow down, the dance must come to an end. The night grows old and weary, but here is this young boy dancing towards the end of the muddy river leaving the ballroom. The angels can weep and the gospels can sing, but no sound can reach here. Ninety-nine… As the poison flows through his veins, his organs begin to chant a cry for mercy, begging for the Lord's blessings, only to fall on deaf ears. His heart becomes numb, his eyes grow heavy as the sun begins to rise and a calm breeze tames the warring river, the music begins to reach its finale for the dance has come to an end. One hundred… "So this is Death?" asks the boy as Persephone guides this lost soul to nothing.

THE WOMAN IN THE YELLOW HAT

It was a quiet day in the summer with a motherly breath of wind prancing in the blue peaceful skies. The lively trees danced over the dwarfed shrubs; even the fallen leaves pranced along the field without a care. It was a ballad of Nature, a sight of beauty, yet ignored by a girl. This girl is dressed in an old-fashioned yellow hat, who comes to the ballad of Nature every day when the ancient, boorish tower roars its song at Three. She always places the same withered blanket on the rigid ground on the same patch of land every day. No matter the weather, no matter the crowd, she always waits for him on the blanket. Never daring to speak a word, her emotions are nothing as she watches the leaves dance to Romantic harmonies of the countryside. As if it were a script in a movie of departure, all who watch and all who hear the song know the man will never come. The man she waits so patiently for resides beneath her feet where a small, cracked stone marks the place of his final resting. For a woman to bear the pain of loving the Dead, she is strong, staying to listen to the Wind's Requiem in D minor. She waits and listens without regret of the past, but blissfully dances in the memories of their love. Once the song ends, she opens her eyes only to realize the dead can no longer hear our heart's screeching cries, for the dead no longer follow the laws of love, and yet she waits, she listens, that woman in the yellow hat.

YOU

It was you.
It was always you.
I believed you.
I loved you.
I want to forget you.
But I still love you.
Hoping.
It will forever be you.

VOICE OF A MONSTER

"Please, please… stay away from me… please—I don't want to die. Help! Can anyone fucking hear me… god damn it… I can't die just yet!" Begging for her life was the woman in the purple dress, her name was Alice, Alice Cartwright. A reserved student studying the laws of man by day, however, when night fell, she shed her innocent look and bloomed into a lustful street performer under the moon's eerie, yet subtly comforting, light. Finding a job wasn't easy; sometimes our bodies are our only source of income.

The image of a person on the brink of death begging for her worthless life… could cause… so much… pleasure. This is the climax I've been yearning for, this is my paradise, I thought to myself. Yes, I might be a terrible person, but we all have our inner demons. In fact, I just can't control it—I just let the voices take over, embracing what humanity really is. That is all.

"Stay away from me, you fucking monster!" she cried out.

"Monster, me, a monster?" Pulling out my butcher knife, which was already soaked in blood from our activities we did at my home, I bent down to look at her in her young brown eyes. I could see the emotions racing through her: confusion, despair, rage, I could go on and on and on, but if I did, I feared I would go berserk and god knew what I would do to this town that had seen no terror.

"Ms. Cartwright, 'monster' is no name fit for a gentleman like myself, however, since I will be the last person you will ever see, I might as well tell you who I am." Holding her fragile, soft, vulnerable neck in the palm of my hand, the thrill of murder began to consume me. With just a little squeeze, and boom, she is no more, to have the power of being the executioner in your hands, such a marvelous feeling if you ask me.

"My name is Viktor Stiens."

News can spread quickly like wildfire with every person adding their own oil to the flames, which creates something that can stray away from the truth or enhance it, as some call it. The island of Harberth, home to around 120,00 civilians, had never understood despair or agony, never witnessed the terrors of war, never heard the cries of the damned. It was an utopia, you could say, an utopia I wished to see burn and suffer. This island needed to understand what it meant to be human, what it meant to be mortal, WHAT IT MEANT TO BE MAD! That was where I came in, the bringer of death, the messenger, not of Zeus, but the messenger of Hades; it was something that was within me that reached nirvana when I witnessed the darkness of humanity.

"Welcome to the bar, Viktor, you want the usual?" asked Bizel. Bizel, a sturdy, towering man who runs the best pub on the island, Gloria Pub, had been a friend of mine since we were kids. He wore the same black coat every day, along with his gray hat. He always smiled, revealing his uneven teeth, but he could care less what people thought of him because he enjoyed his life at the moment.

"Yeah… how have you been recently, Biz, how's the kids?" I asked.

"I've been alright, Viktor, the pub's doing alright, making me some good money. Who knows, I might open a second one across the island to reach the northern parts. The kids are just being kids, nothing out of the ordinary. My oldest daughter, Alexsia, is back in town so there's that," responded Biz.

"Hey, can you turn up the radio, Biz? Some shit went down on 13th Street," screamed a customer across the pub.

I took a sip of my drink with the slightest of grins, knowing what had transpired last night…. *I still can't get over those eyes, her screams, ahhh…. her desperate cries that echoed in the night…. 21… 23… 19,* I thought to myself while passing the radio to Biz.

"This just in citizens of Harberth island, I am stricken by grief to announce that authorities have discovered another body on the intersection of 12th and 13th Street across the harbor. The body is identified as Alice Cartwright who was a 19-year-old college student studying law. Her body was found in a dark alleyway curled into a ball with 21 stab wounds, 23 deep slashes, her fingers chopped off, her eyes removed, and 19 stab wounds to the head. This is the eight reported body found in the past two weeks, and as a result, authorities are placing a mandatory curfew on the whole island no matter your age or class. The curfew will start at 10:30 p.m., and any person or persons outside after this designated time will be promptly arrested and fined. Please be safe, please be cautious, this is your local news. Thank you."

The pub became silent, the once lively crowd telling tales of their past while dreaming of their future could only think of the terrors that Alice witnessed in her final hours. The atmosphere became dull, and the air was filled with sorrow and grief for her and her family. It was hard to breathe. My mouth felt as if I were out in the deserts of the Pharaoh, gasping for water.

"Hey, Viktor, what kind of monster would do such a thing to an innocent girl?" asked Biz, holding back his tears of rage. I could understand his pain with him being the father of two girls; just the idea of any harm violating a man's daughter would create a rageful beast.

"Monster, you know monsters don't exist, Bizel. In fact, any man can do such crimes if you push him far enough off the edge," I calmly replied.

"But for a man to do such crimes repeatedly, it's as if he or she had thrown away their humanity and signed a deal with the devil… in order to become an ang—"

"An angel of death, that has a good ring to it, Biz. Well anyways, thanks for the drinks, you can keep the change. I'm going for a walk then home."

I'm starting to lose control over my impulses, this desire of mine to witness pain, to inflict pain…. it's just too much! This addiction is now creeping into my daily life at work, at home, at the pub…. I need another one, yes, another Alice or Mary or Sondra. I NEED MORE. Pondering over these unholy desires of mine, I somehow wandered off to Harberth Park in the center of the island and there she was.

A beautiful, charming, delicate, graceful, elegant young woman singing under the moonlight, her hair dancing along to her heavenly voice flowing with majestic ease with assistance from the calm, quiet breeze. Even the trees were dancing along to her performance. Her goldish, long, free, soft hair flying through the sky, her blue eyes gleaming in the night, she was the embodiment of beauty and mystery. *This has to be destiny*, I thought to myself as I slowly approached her. *Of course, it IS our destiny to meet.*

"Excuse me, young lady, what are you doing here alone at night?" I asked. She looked at me with a blank expression, her eyes pierced right through me as she continued her song.

"You know it's dangerous out here at night, because once night falls, man shows his true colors while god is sleeping." Again, no response from her, but I couldn't look away, not even for a split second. She ended her song and finally looked down to me as if she were an angel from the heavens pitying me for being a mortal human.

"You're the killer, aren't you?" she asked.

"What did you say…"

HOW DOES SHE KNOW! This has to be a joke or something…. There were no witnesses those nights, I even made sure of it. I could only laugh at her ridiculous, bold question; however, her demeanor didn't change; her once majestic, innocent look turned into disgust. She was serious.

"You're starting to sweat, mister, even your legs are starting to shake a little. So I am right, you are the killer, the angel of Death as some call it." Glaring into my eyes with no expression at all, I couldn't make her out at all, no emotions raced through her at all. The mysterious woman started to approach me as she whistled Chopin's funeral march. I even felt chills running rampant across my body.

Kill, kill, kill, kill, kill, kill, that's all I could think about in that moment, this overwhelming feeling began to consume me. *Imagine her screams, imagine her cries, imagine her fighting, and best of all, that doll-like, blank face of hers… it could be my new masterpiece… imagine the face she would make…ahhhhh.* I couldn't control myself much longer, but I knew this was not the opportunity to do this. This could be a trap; if so, I would get caught and executed. *Slaughter her… dissect her,* I thought to myself.

"To accuse me of such crimes, I should have the honor of knowing your name, young lady."

"Alexsia Gordon, daughter of Bizreal Gordon." As soon as she responded, a powerful wind blew by as if the soloist of the concerto had reached the climax of the piece. Glorious.

"Look, I don't know what you're talking about, Alexsia. I didn't do anyt—"

"You were wearing the same mask my father bought for your now deceased son, Mathew's, birthday ten years ago. The half white and black one that represents balance and tranquility, but now it has a crack over the right eye socket because Ms. Alice kicked you in the face right over the eye while you tried to pin her down. Trust me, I saw everything that happened.

She… saw… everything, I thought to myself. No one would've known about those specific details unless they were there to witness the crime. *I have to get rid of her…. I have to get rid of her.*

The moon, reaching its peak in the lonely, dark sky, over-looked us like a lion stalking his prey. I knew I had to get rid of her, but this haunting idea floated around in my head, which began to eat away at my already dark conscious. She was the daughter of my best friend. I still had my old pistol in my pocket; my fingers began to dance with the handle of the old rusty gun as if Chopin were playing a ballad for us.

Kill, kill, kill, kill, kill, that was all I could think about, that was all I could fucking think about.

"You sure do know a lot about me, my crimes, my life, my secrets, my motives, and so on. So you know what I must do to you… right?" I responded to her as I approached her calmly; still my fingers continued to dance with the old rusty pistol in my pocket. Everything around us was becoming still, calm, quiet, transparent. If you listened to the winds parading around us, you could hear the whispers of the gods, the whispers of the angels and demons. I could hear them singing to me.

I pulled the gun out of my pocket and aimed right for her head. My eyes knew who she was and what she meant to Bizreal, but mentally I only saw a shadow figure in front of me that knew my secrets, a figure that I knew I must destroy. She began to approach me, grabbed the gun, and pointed the barrel right to her head.

"Alexsia! Alexsia!" I could hear a man screaming off into the distance, his voice grew closer and closer to the park. *I can't have any more witnesses, I have to pull the DAMN trigger. No, don't pull the fucking trigger, she IS Bizreal's daughter.* My thoughts began to argue with each other like an elderly couple fighting over the simplest of things. No, don't pull the trigger. Yes, pull the trigger now and run into the night. Be free.

As soon as I was about to pull the trigger, I heard a man scream my name; it was a voice that my ears and soul were familiar with, a voice that this town loved along with his pub, a voice I called my best friend. It was Bizreal.

"Viktor, what are you doing with my daughter?"

"You know, it's a shame that you caught me in this state, I promise it is not what you thi—"

"Step away from my daughter, now."

"She knows I can't do tha—"

"VIKTOR, STEP AWAY FROM MY FUCKING DAUGH-TER!" His voice rippled through the sky and interrupted the waltz between the winds and the trees. Reaching into his coat pocket, he pulled out a pump action shotgun, the same one he keeps behind the bar just in case things got a little disturbing.

"Viktor, I will shoot if you don't move away from my daughter." He slowly approached us.

"Fine… fine… fine," I calmly stated as I slowly backed away from her and nodded my head towards Bizreal as a sign for her to leave to her guardian angel. As he lowered his gun preparing to embrace his eldest daughter, I suddenly grabbed her by the arm and held her body in front of mine, utilizing her as a human shield. I could feel her warm body, her soft skin, her pure, delightful smell danced around my noise. I pointed the gun to the side of her head and cracked a small, yet not so innocent, more like devilish, smile. Bizreal cocked his shotgun and had the eyes of a real killer, a real monster, a real devil.

"Remember what I said in the bar, Bizreal, 'Monster, you know monsters don't exist, Bizel. In fact, any man can do such crimes if you push him far enough off the edge.' Well look at you right now, Bizreal."

"Viktor, this is no time for your fucking games, death is not a fucking game, life is not a fucking game, this is reality, wake up!" His desperate cries could be heard across the whole island.

I could tell both God and the Devil himself were watching from their respective seats above man, I could tell the angels circling us like vultures singing their gospels in hope of a happy ending, in the hope of a miracle.

"Game... you think... I think this is a game?" I responded. I was getting ready to explode, *kill, kill, kill, kill, kill, kill,* my mind was becoming cloudy, muddy, dark, a bottomless pit of wrath and unimaginable rage. "Bizreal, I confess my sins to you my friend, I am the bringer of death to this island, I am the Angel of the Dead. I killed them all and you know what... I ENJOYED EVERY BIT OF IT! I love their screams, I love the smell of fresh blood oozing out of a dead body, I love the struggle. I killed 57: women, children, men, the old, the young, the healthy, the dying, I even killed the INFANTS! No one is safe from death, not even this fake utopia we all call home, this is REALITY!" *My final speech I will ever preach to an audience... was beautiful,* I thought to myself.

I stepped away from Alexsia, releasing her to her worried guardian angel as I gazed upon the full moon above me. The dark, yet peaceful, moonlight sonata began to play in my head. A sigh of relief came over me as I could see the angels preparing my chariot to the afterlife where the gods and demons could judge my destroyed mind.

This is a good ending to my nightmare, I thought to myself.

"Bizreal!" I shouted out to him. "If god created every-thing and knows everything that will happen... why did he create a monster like me... why did he create evil?" Before he could give a preacher-worthy response, I raised the gun to my head, the dance between the trigger and my fingers finally came to its finale.

Bang.

A SOLDIER'S LETTER

For those who cannot, I stand strong for her

Not knowing what the future holds; I fight

With every soul that fought, their name a blur

Our wounded flag soars, a beautiful sight

Bombarding bombs, I dream a world anew

To my heart never sending our kids to hell I wake, as the
sky is no longer blue I am afraid to tell, afraid to yell.

But this is for not I, but for thy soul

It's not about my wants, but for her needs

To come home to you for another stroll It's our duty to do
our nation's deeds. To fight for those at home I pray to you to
return to my love, to say I do.

Abandon My Own Companion?

Watching, waiting, desiring increase

A tale of a woman who I hold dear

Fighting beasts, my fractured heart rests in peace.

May I not love; ridiculed by my fear.

To say that we cannot be, I trust thee

You dance with an illusion, hiding pain

Rejecting a knight's hand, how could this be?

It is your bidding that you let him reign

Pity; prancing from partner to partner

It's nothing but shame, I could reject fame

To most, nothing more than a foreigner

As I lay in bed, I burn in aflame

Why do I believe your my companion

My love for you will never abandon.

GOD FORGIVE ME FOR I HAVE SINNED

Misery is nothing but a disease
A parasite fit for a ruthless king,
I pray my final breath will come with ease
That the old will blossom new unto Spring.
As I lay to ache, waiting for my fate
Welcoming, I dream of a world no more.
I wish to meet her, and yet I must wait
To rage against myself; I charge to war.
Dear God hear my cries, hear my dreadful cries
I dare not harm God's greatest benign gift
Afraid time is gone to face my demise
I face you allowing my mind to drift.
Shame; no money can buy a homicide
A baffled man compelled with suicide.

REALIZATION

People, we thrive in Greed, we thrive in fear
Our planet is nothing as she once was.
The crowd holds ambitions, their wants, unclear
Humankind, we blindly dance in his jaws.
Materials, money, fame, without shame
Climbing, utilizing the poor such whores
How can we preach when no one takes the blame
The young sent to die in their father's wars
Could it be that we are destined to fail
Could it be that we are demons from hell
Could it be that we are convicts in jail
Should we all rest, prepare our last farewell
Even so this world is a nightmare to some
As I lay, I dream the next day will come

LIFE OF A POET

BIRTH

To be welcomed, two beings I know not
I cry, I scream from darkness, I see light.
A newborn flower blooms, a sight they thought;
Spite of me they smile, fearful I might
To be named, I understand not a sound
I squirm like a bug as I learn movement
They smiled, this infant fool who was crowned
The peaceful fresh air, what an improvement
Who am I, what am I, Why was I born?
Struggle to breath, should I exist with ease?
Another life is given, shall we mourn?
Who allowed me to exist, this disease?
I was picked to be born, a tragedy to be,
I hold a soul of agony.

LIFE

I am who I am, I am what I am
I; nothing more than a swarm of atoms
Poisoned by the plague, follow thy program
I wish to hide, my vision like Tatum's
It is hard to live a life, to be free
The world says be happy, to yell for joy
Isn't life marvelous, don't you agree?
Conquer life, like the men who conquered Troy!
Just be happy, just make friends they all say
Just live your life we all only have one
Just take this fucking world on day by day
Just be; don't be another anyone
For those who preach to me of better times
I must pray to God; prepare for my crimes

SUICIDE

I sit here, knowing I am doomed to hell
I sit here not as your equal, never.
I sit here, preparing for my dispel
I sit here, welcome, darkness forever
I pray to you as I write my farewells
I ask for your forgiveness I beg, Lord
I wish I could enjoy the season bells
But my cries, my pain, all of it; ignored
I sit here with nothing more than a gun
I sit here, I rest my pen for the end
I sit here, yearning for the holy sun
I sit here, knowing my soul will descend
To say I have failed as your creation
I hereby sentence thee to damnation

DEATH

The act, done, my final poem complete
I fall to the flames as I watch Cobain
The world of fire, what awaits this heat
At last maybe I am free from thy pain
Nero, Bennington, Robin, and now I
We all fell to our demise, suicide
I beg the world of the living, don't cry
I killed myself, while having zero pride
What caused this, why would one choose to die, why?
Ask my body, ask the dead why this fate.
All of you, everyone, you, just stood by
Now you ask, you ask, I disintegrate
I wish I could be or what If I knew
To look at me I should yell, I love you

THE WITCH

I swear to thee, that my life is for you to stand,
I shall never forsake thy name.
May I dare say I believe God must knew,
to call me Joan I shall swallow thy blame.
For the enraged crowd begs for your demise
They chant, they cry, demanding your true crime
Amongst them I stare, I seek to the skies
Treat her like a witch we shall pay in time.
I fear that my actions will cause my end
To protect the vile witch is high treason
However I shall not falter my friend
There is no just here, a tragic season.
I swear you are no witch, but a true Queen
My love is boundless, it knows no between

ONLY IN DREAMS

Easy to say love, without having love. Is it pain or sadness that holds me hostage, I think not, an emptiness would be better.

A walk down a snowy night, arms locked Together, rivals any gift my parents could Offer. So it seems, only in dreams.

My heart doesn't ache from my past mistakes,

Or regrets. No… actually I never experienced her, Misery, from love. But my chest still yearns for some form of Comfort, some form of attention.

Enjoying the warmth from this cozy wooden fire,

Cuddling under the rigid blanket, nobody dare say

Anything could compare. So it seems… Only in dreams.

So what is this feeling… this tight feeling where my heart rests,

If it's not me suffering from the lost of love, then could it be…

No, it can't be a lost love, rather it's the fact I never experienced

Love. (Is love that important for us humans?)

The word *love*, a basic word known to all, yet only experienced by a lucky few. Maybe I could experience this enigma and call someone my own. Someday.

Until then, my love rests in my dreams.

FALSE PEACE

The trees of the Southern land guarded thee,

As the birds harmonized on heaven's door

I stood watching the animals run free.

Who knew that life can offer so much more.

Blinding, clouded by my sacred devil

I finally witnessed a miracle

Standing, preaching his name; mister Bevile.

Nurturing, the music was lyrical.

Finally taming the beast we call life,

With beaded eyes I see this viscous world.

The pain of my mind struck by a dull knife,

such an evil sight yet the water purled.

Peace is all I wanted in general,

who knew it could live at your funeral.

COURAGE OF NATURE

Blinding like the sun on a summer's day,
Her locks of orange, brown soaring in the sky,
her lashes dance among the winds of May.
She draws my heart into a troubled fray.
I gawk into her eyes of bitter snow, rivaling the sun,
Aelia too stares.
Her soothing warmth that I shall never know,
She dances with the bees sharing no care.
I trust nature's beauty shall never fade,
To live where your love is lost in a dream,
To say my only love has been betrayed,
I lay amongst the leaves heading downstream
Until I am able to stand and see
I wish my passion can give life to thee

AN ABSENT LOVE

Easy to say love without having love
Wish to be found with some delicate hope,
The bird of love I wish to fly, a dove, yet dictating like a
useless old pope.
With the sessions of regretful lonely thought
Summoning memories of my quiet past,
Pondering over very things I sought, Fearing my tragic love
will never last.
I weep with them in the calm night
I wonder if these anxious thoughts are my foe, a scream of
anguish with no one in sight, ashamed to carry a burden of
woes. But maybe while I think of you, my friend, all losses are
not, my sorrows can end